D0604410

DISCARDED
NATIONAL CITY LIBRARY

BABY FOR SALE

by Jackie French Koller
illustrated by Janet Pedersen

MARSHALL CAVENDISH   NEW YORK

THIS BOOK IS THE PROPERTY OF
THE NATIONAL CITY PUBLIC LIBRARY
1401 NATIONAL CITY BLVD
NATIONAL CITY, CA 91950

Text copyright 2002 © by Jackie French Koller
Illustrations copyright 2002 © by Janet Pedersen
All rights reserved.
Marshall Cavendish, 99 White Plains Road, Tarrytown, NY 10591

Library of Congress Cataloging-in-Publication Data
Koller, Jackie French.
Baby for sale / by Jackie French Koller ; illustrations by Janet Pedersen.
   p.   cm.
Summary: When Peter feels he cannot put up with his baby sister Emily any
longer, he puts her in his wagon and goes around the block to see if any of
the neighbors want to buy her.
ISBN 0-7614-5106-4
[1. Brothers and sisters--Fiction. 2. Babies--Fiction.] I.Pedersen, Janet. II. Title.
PZ7.K833 Bab 2002   [E]--dc21   2001047171

The text of this book is set in 15 point Esprit Book
The illustrations are rendered in watercolors.
Printed in Malaysia   First edition.
6 5 4 3 2 1

To Jack, who is Priceless! — J.F.K.

For John and Delores — J.P.

It was the last straw. Peter had never made a fuss about his baby sister Emily drooling on his toys or ripping his books. For over a year he had put up with her awful smells, and very loud yells, and the terrible messes she made with her food. He hadn't even complained when she learned to walk and started following him everywhere. But now she had taken his brand new baseball cap and thrown it in the toilet!

There was only one thing to do. Peter lifted Emily into his wagon and started off down the block.

"Baby for sale!" he shouted. "Baby for sale!"

Before long he came upon Mrs. LaPlante, working
in her garden.

"Would you like to buy a baby?" Peter asked.

Mrs. LaPlante sat back on her heels.
"Now why would I want a baby?"
she asked.

"Her skin is soft like a rose," he said, stroking Emily's cheek with his finger, "and her mouth is—Ouch!"

Mrs. LaPlante laughed. "Um, I have all the roses I need, thank you," she said, "and mine don't bite!"

Peter pulled his finger out of Emily's mouth. "No!" he shouted, shaking his finger at her from a safe distance.

Emily shook her finger back at him.

"You're *not* cute," said Peter, and off he went once more, shouting, "Baby for sale! Baby for sale!"

Next he came upon Mr. Diaz's antique shop. Mr. Diaz was setting up a display on the sidewalk. "Would you like to buy a baby?" Peter asked.

Mr. Diaz straightened up and looked at Emily. "Why would a bachelor like me want a baby?" he asked.

Peter thought again. "When you tickle her tummy, she makes a happy sound," he said.

Crash! Bang! Plinkety plunk!
"Oh no!" cried Peter. Emily had
grabbed Mr. Diaz's tablecloth.
Antiques were flying everywhere!
Peter snatched Emily out of the
way of a toppling lamp.

Mr. Diaz scowled. "*That* is not my idea of a happy sound!" he said. "Please take that baby away from here!"

Emily put Mr. Diaz's tablecloth over her head.
"Peek-a-boo," she said. Peter rolled his eyes.

Next, Peter came to Mrs. Stengle's convenience store. He pushed
the door open. "Would you like to buy a baby?" he called.

Out came Mrs. Stengle. "A baby?" she said. "What would I do with
a baby?"

"You can talk to her," said
Peter, "and she'll talk back."
He knelt beside Emily. "Say *Peter*,"
he told her.

"Poo-pee," said Emily, tugging
on her diaper.

"Oh no," said Peter.

Mrs. Stengle laughed. "Lucky for you
I'm running a sale on diapers," she said.

"Peeyew," said Peter as he helped Mrs.
Stengle change Emily. "She's still for sale,"
he said hopefully when they were done.

"Sorry," said Mrs. Stengle. "When
I want someone to talk to,
I think I'll just call
a friend."

"No more pooping!" said Peter as he put Emily back in the wagon.

Emily grinned. "No mo poopee," she repeated.

Peter tried hard not to laugh. "Cut it out," he said. Off he went, pulling the wagon once more. Soon he came upon a street musician.

"Baby for sale," said Peter. "Would you like to buy a baby?"

The musician made up a little song and sang it for Emily.

"Pretty little baby blue,
What in the world would I do with you?"

"You could sing for her," said Peter, "and she would clap." He bent down and clapped his hands in front of Emily. "Clap hands," he said. Emily grabbed his nose.

" Thop that!" cried Peter.

The musician laughed. "I think I'll just let the people on the street clap for me," he said.

"Emily!" said Peter, rubbing his nose. "That hurts!" Emily giggled and clapped her hands.

Peter sighed and shook his head.

By the time Peter got to the end of the block, Emily was getting cranky. Mrs. Chang was sitting in one of the rocking chairs on the front porch of the Rose Arbor Inn. Peter pulled the wagon up her front walk. He carried Emily onto the porch and sat down in an empty chair next to Mrs. Chang.

"Would you like to buy a baby?" he asked.

"Now what in the world would an old woman like me do with a baby?" said Mrs. Chang.

"You could rock her like this," said Peter, rocking the struggling baby back and forth, "and she'd fall asleep in your lap." Emily kicked and squirmed until Peter had to let her down. She toddled off after Mrs. Chang's cat.

Mrs. Chang laughed. "My cat falls asleep in my lap," she said. "I really don't need a baby."

"Are you sure?" said Peter. "She can do lots of cute things. She can walk and talk and clap her hands."

"Sorry," said Mrs. Chang.

Peter sighed. "Nobody needs a baby," he said.

"Maybe not," said Mrs. Chang, "but I'd say that baby needs you. Look!"

"Oh no!" cried Peter.

Emily had climbed down the steps and was toddling along the walk toward the street. And a car was coming!

"Emily!" Peter shouted. But Emily didn't stop. She just giggled and kept right on going. Peter jumped down the stairs and raced after her. Emily giggled louder and toddled faster.

Peter reached her just as
she was about to step off the
curb. He grabbed her up and held
her tight as the car zoomed by. Peter's
heart banged like a drum. Emily kicked
and fussed but Peter just held her and held her.

Mrs. Chang came down the walk, pulling the wagon.
Peter sat Emily down in it.

"Don't you ever run away like that again," he told her,
then he kissed her on the cheek.

Emily puckered her lips and made a little kissing sound
in return.

Peter smiled.

"You know what else Emily can do?" Peter said to Mrs. Chang.

"What?" asked Mrs. Chang.

"She can wave good-bye," said Peter. "Wave good-bye, Emily,"

Emily opened and closed her little fist. "Bye-bye," she said as Peter turned the wagon towards home.